W9-ARG-192

APR 1 7 2009

Withdrawn

MAY 0 5 2009
MAY 1 8 2009

JUN 1 8 2009

JUL 0 6 2009

JUL 2 7 2009

AUG 0 5 2009

SEP 0 3 2009

NOV 0 9 2009

MAR 2 0 2009

Northville District Library
212 W. Cady Street
Northville, MI 48167-1560

Dear Parent:

Congratulations! Your child is taking the first steps on an exciting journey. The destination? Independent reading!

STEP INTO READING® will help your child get there. The program offers five steps to reading success. Each step includes fun stories and colorful art. There are also Step into Reading Sticker Books, Step into Reading Math Readers, Step into Reading Write-In Readers, Step into Reading Phonics Readers, and Step into Reading Phonics First Steps! Boxed Sets—a complete literacy program with something for every child.

Learning to Read, Step by Step!

Ready to Read   Preschool–Kindergarten
• **big type and easy words** • **rhyme and rhythm** • **picture clues**
For children who know the alphabet and are eager to begin reading.

Reading with Help   Preschool–Grade 1
• **basic vocabulary** • **short sentences** • **simple stories**
For children who recognize familiar words and sound out new words with help.

Reading on Your Own   Grades 1–3
• **engaging characters** • **easy-to-follow plots** • **popular topics**
For children who are ready to read on their own.

Reading Paragraphs   Grades 2–3
• **challenging vocabulary** • **short paragraphs** • **exciting stories**
For newly independent readers who read simple sentences with confidence.

Ready for Chapters   Grades 2–4
• **chapters** • **longer paragraphs** • **full-color art**
For children who want to take the plunge into chapter books but still like colorful pictures.

STEP INTO READING® is designed to give every child a successful reading experience. The grade levels are only guides. Children can progress through the steps at their own speed, developing confidence in their reading, no matter what their grade.

Remember, a lifetime love of reading starts with a single step!

For Laura and Peter, with love
—A.S.C.

For Bonnie and Lola, with love
—K.W.

Text copyright © 2008 by Alyssa Satin Capucilli
Illustrations copyright © 2008 by Kay Widdowson

All rights reserved.
Published in the United States by Random House Children's Books,
a division of Random House, Inc., New York.

Step into Reading, Random House, and the Random House colophon
are registered trademarks of Random House, Inc.

Visit us on the Web!
www.stepintoreading.com

Educators and librarians, for a variety of teaching tools, visit us at
www.randomhouse.com/teachers

Library of Congress Cataloging-in-Publication Data
Capucilli, Alyssa Satin.
Panda kisses / by Alyssa Satin Capucilli ; illustrated by Kay Widdowson. — 1st ed.
    p.   cm. — (Step into reading. Step 1)
Summary: A panda cub tries to find out what kind of kiss is just right for him,
with help from his parents.
ISBN 978-0-375-84562-8 (pbk.) — ISBN 978-0-375-94562-5 (lib. bdg.)
[1. Stories in rhyme. 2. Kissing—Fiction. 3. Parent and child—Fiction. 4. Pandas—Fiction.
5. China—Fiction.] I. Widdowson, Kay, ill. II. Title.
PZ8.3.C1935Pan 2008
[E]—dc22   2008001574

Printed in the United States of America

10 9 8 7 6 5 4 3 2 1

First Edition

Random House Children's Books supports the First Amendment and celebrates the right to read.

Panda Kisses

by Alyssa Satin Capucilli

illustrated by Kay Widdowson

Random House New York

Mother Bear,
I want a kiss!

A soft kiss?

A sweet kiss?

A sticky bamboo
treat kiss?

Father Bear,
I want a kiss!

A low kiss?

A high kiss?

A climb up

to the sky kiss?

How about a sunny kiss?

How about a bunny kiss?

A fish kiss?

A flower kiss?

Or a cool
sun shower kiss?

What other kisses
can there be?
I must find
the one for me.

A kiss

inside a silk cocoon?

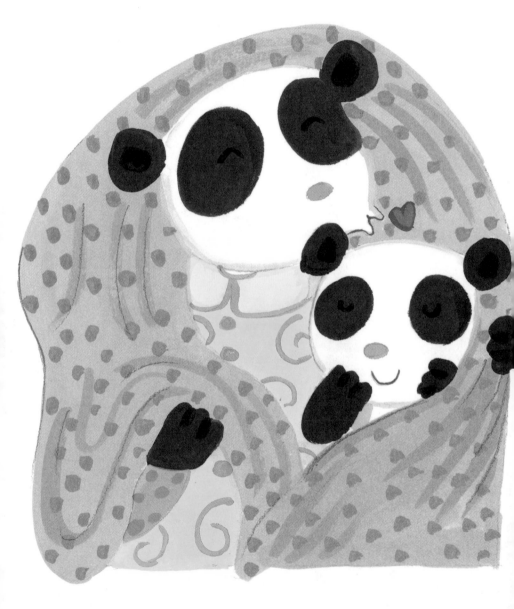

A kiss

under a big full moon?

WAIT!

There are many kisses
that will do!

But the best kiss is—
from both of you!

31